GW01086454

Nia and the Mermaids

STEPHANIE O'CONNOR

Copyright © 2020 Stephanie O'Connor

All rights reserved.

No part of this book may be reproduced in any
form or by any means, electronic, mechanical,
photocopying, recording or otherwise, without
the prior written permission of the publisher,
except by reviewers, who may quote brief
passages in a review.

ISBN: 979-8-67633-316-4

ALSO BY STEPHANIE O'CONNOR

Ayman
Matthew and the Tiger
The Little Bat Who Loved Halloween
First Flight
Nia and the Mermaids
Rocco Molloy - Giggle Doctor
The Tree Days of Christmas
Maria's Painting

The Fox in the Suitcase Series:
Lucy's Encyclopedia (Book 1)
Ben's Studies (Book 2)
The Boy Who Liked to Run (Book 3)
The Golden Sunflowers (Book 4)

CONTENTS

NIA AND THE MERMAIDS

For Isabella and Matthew

CHAPTER 1
NIA'S BUCKET LIST

"Nobody's ever seen a mermaid," said Nia's mom, "except perhaps in the movies."

"Why not?" asked Nia, looking intently up into her mom's face.

They were sitting at the kitchen table, looking out of the window, and across the harbour at the rolling blue waves of the Atlantic.

Their house, a small white cottage was built on a cliff, overlooking a pretty bay, on the west coast of Ireland. Her mom often said they were lucky to have such a lovely home. It had been built by her father, Nia's grandpa, who had once lived there happily with his family. That was a long time before Nia was born. When Nia knew her grandpa, he had been an old man, and he had adored his little granddaughter. It was Nia's grandpa who had taught her to love the sea, and they had been constant companions right up to the day he died.

"Why hasn't anybody seen a mermaid?" asked Nia again.

"'Well, because mermaids aren't real," replied her mom.

"But if no one's seen them, how do they know they aren't real?" replied the young girl.

"Hmm, good question" her mom replied, slowly nodding her head, "I guess you better keep your eyes open this summer. Maybe you'll be the first to spot one."

Nia was thoughtful for a moment.

"Well, I hope I do see a mermaid someday, and if I do, I'm going to swim with her," she said.

"That would be lovely," said her mom seriously, "but you'd have to be very careful because they're excellent swimmers. Remember they're not like you or me, mermaids are half fish and the ocean is their world, and they use their great fins for swimming down deep into the water."

"Have they got arms?" asked Nia.

"Oh yes, they're supposed to have arms just like you. And their hair is long and silky and floats all around them in the water. And sometimes when they come up to the top of the waves, they jump up onto rocks to sit in the sunshine and sing songs that go right to your heart like magic."

"But if no one's seen them, then how do you know?" asked the young girl, looking up into her moms face with big, round eyes.

"Know what?"

"About their fins, about their silky hair and magic songs."

Her mom laughed. She got up out of her chair to clear the plates from the table, then she stopped for a moment and put a hand on her daughter's shoulders.

"What's so funny?" demanded Nia. "How does anybody know about mermaids if they've never seen them?" Nia asked again.

"They don't know, I guess." her mom answered, smiling.

Nia thought this over. "Somebody *must* have seen them," she declared positively.

"Maybe," her mom answered thoughtfully.

Nia loved her mom with all her heart and believed she was the smartest person in the world, but she certainly wasn't making much sense about mermaids!

"How do mermaids live?" she asked. "in caves, or just in water like fish, or how?"

"Oh, now, that I don't know," her mom replied. "I'm guessing they have houses and maybe there are cities down there."

"Wow," she said, "their homes must be very pretty."

"And very wet."

"I'd like to be a mermaid, mom," said the child earnestly.

"What, and live in the sea?" her mom exclaimed.

"Well, just for one day," Nia replied.

CHAPTER 2

THE MERMAIDS

The next morning, as soon as Nia had finished breakfast and helped her mom with the dishes, the two of them set off towards the beach.

The sky was blue, and the air was warm. As they followed the narrow winding path that led down to the beach below and approached the shore, they watched the edges of the gentle waves sparkle in the sun. Across the bay, they could see the fisherman's boats trawling for the daily catch.

Nia loved the sea, and the beach was her favourite place to go where she could spend entire days exploring. And how much had she to explore and play with! The entire seashore, for miles, was covered with playthings for her—sand perfect for castles with moats; pebbles of every shade of grey, yellow, amber, and white, polished by the sea and smooth and round to touch. Not to mention rock pools with tiny crabs, and the slippery shining seaweed among the rocks—all were exiting to explore to the young girl.

How well she remembered all the old stories her grandpa had told her about shipwrecks and pirates. As she collected stones and shells, she would imagine whole scenes as if in a movie, that the pebbles in her fingers were jewels washed upon the shore from shipwrecks.

It never once occurred to her to that her days were lonely and boring because there was so much to see and do at the beach. To Nia, the ocean itself was like a great book; and every day she read a new page in it—the calm water, the swell of the sea, the breeze and choppy waves of the storm.

Soon Nia and her mom reached the sand and walked to their usual sheltered spot just beneath an overhanging rock face. Nia grabbed her float and ran to the water edge and began paddling.

"It's warm," she shouted back to her mom. "Can I go explore the caves?"

"Okay. But be careful in the water," her mom answered.

And so Nia happily started to paddle around the short distance towards the north of the headland, and towards the caves.

Nia loved exploring the beach caves. Many of them opened right at the water's edge, and it was possible to walk far into their dark depths. The largest one was called *Smuggler's Cave*, and her mom had told her that a long time ago, smugglers used to hide things in it.

Nia continued, dreamily, trailing her feet as she slowly moved through the water, and soon began to feel the sun's heat on her shoulders.

"I wonder if mermaids ever go into Smuggler's Cave?" she thought just as she reached the archway through which the water flowed. She had been to this cave many times before with her mom and knew that when the tide was low, as it was at that moment, it was safe to go into the cave.

"I think I'll explore," she thought. "Besides, it'll be cooler in there than out here in the sun."

As soon as she entered the big black archway that marked its entrance, she felt the cool air on her skin, and the water was calm and cold on her feet. As she slowly walked further into the dim interior of the cave, the only sound she could hear was the gentle lapping of the water against the sides of the cave walls.

It was just as she moved forward a little further in, that a beautiful sight met her eyes, and Nia was struck dumb with amazement.

Although she was quite a way into the cave, it was not dark, if anything, it was lighter here than at the entrance, and the light seemed to come from underneath the water, which glowed all around her with a beautiful turquoise colour. Slowly Nia moved a little farther into the dim interior of the vast cave, and looked around, amazed at the unexpected beauty of the water hidden away.

"Hello," said a sweet voice.

Nia gave a start and looked around, but there was no one there. Looking down at the water just beside her she saw little circles within circles.

"Is someone there?" she whispered cautiously, and then stared, for there right before her eyes and rising from the turquoise water was a face, then shoulders around which floated a mass of long, black hair. It was a girl's face, not much older than herself, and the eyes smiled kindly. Suddenly there was a second face, this time surrounded by a mass of floating brown hair.

"Are you — mermaids?" asked Nia curiously. She was not a bit afraid. They seemed both gentle and friendly.

"Yes," both answered together.

"And you live here — in Smuggler's Cave?" asked an amazed Nia.

"Here and there," replied the one with the black hair, "We live in the ocean and move about."

When they spoke, their voices sounded sweet and clear, and their tones were very gentle.

While the young girl stared at them for a few moments, they examined her in return with considerable curiosity.

"Can you guess why we have appeared to you?" said the other mermaid with brown hair, coming nearer and rising until her neck and shoulders showed plainly above the water.

"Why?" asked Nia.

"Because we like to meet land girls our age," said the black-haired mermaid.

"And we heard you say yesterday you would like to see a mermaid, and so we decided to grant your wish." said the other mermaid.

"That's very nice of you," said Nia gratefully, "but how did you hear me?"

"We have powers that allow us to hear what we wish," said the brown-haired mermaid.

"Also, we wanted to prove to you that we *do* exist!" they both said together.

"I just knew you would," said Nia.

The mermaids spun in the water, and the cave was filled with happy laughter, and when they stopped, Nia said,

"May I see your tales, please? Are they green with scales like a fish?"

The two mermaids turned and looked at each other and seemed undecided as to what to say to this. They both swam a little way off, where they put their heads together and talked for a moment or two before coming back to where Nia stood.

"Would you like to visit our home and see all the wonders that exist below the ocean?" the black-haired mermaid asked.

"Really? I absolutely would," replied Nia promptly, "but I can't. If I go under the water, I might drown."

"Oh no," said the first mermaid. "We would make you like one of us, and then you could live within the water as easily as we do."

"You can really do that? " said Nia.

"Yes, and you don't need to stay with us a moment longer than you want to," replied the mermaid, smiling. "Whenever you want to return home, we promise we will bring you right back here and restore to you the same human form you are now."

"So I would have a fish's tail like you?" asked Nia.

"No. You would have a *mermaid's* tail like us," was the reply.

Nia stood on the rock undecided what to do. Never in her life had she been more bewildered and excited by the strangeness of this adventure she had encountered. At first, she could hardly believe it was all true and that she was not dreaming; but there in the water, real live mermaids were floating about right in front of her eyes!

"I want to," said Nia. "I want to know how you live. But I'm scared."

"There's no danger," insisted the black-haired mermaid.

"Don't you believe us?" asked the mermaid, "Perhaps you are afraid to trust us to bring you back safely to this cave?"

"If you are afraid, you mustn't come." said the brown-haired mermaid "We simply thought you might like to see our beautiful home."

"But I do. I'd love to see everything," said Nia, her eyes glistening with excitement.

"Then come with us,"

"Okay," Nia decided, "I'm going to accept and go with you. What shall I do? Just jump into the water?"

"Give me your hand," answered the black-haired mermaid, lifting her arm from the water, and Nia took her hand, which was warm and soft.

"My name is Sirena," continued the mermaid, "and this is my sister, Coralia."

Suddenly, there came a strange lightness to Nia's legs, and she had a great longing to be in the water. Just then, there was a splash, and Nia caught a gleam of green scales, and the next moment she was in the water with the mermaids, and laughing with joy.

CHAPTER 3

THE DEEP BLUE OCEAN

As they swam through the water Nia was having so much fun and was amazed at all the things she could do. She could dart around in the water this way and that, and with incredible speed. She could turn and dive, and leap about in the water - things she could never have imagined being able to do on land.

And the strangest thing about it was - the water didn't even seem to make her wet! Because although she was underneath the surface of the water, the material of her swimsuit still seemed dry and warm - just as it had been when she walked on the beach in the sunlight a little earlier.

Best of all was when she ducked underwater she could see everything around her just as clearly as she had ever seen anything above water. When she looked back over her shoulder, she could even see the motion of her new mermaid tail, all covered with pretty green scales, which gleamed like jewels. And she noticed now that the mermaids were wearing clothes too. Their beautiful gowns seemed to be made of a material that was like silk, with wide flowing sleeves and trains that sparked and floated far behind the mermaids as they swam. Nia was fascinated and noticed that they also wore strings of beautiful pearls around their necks and wrists. But they didn't wear any jewellery in their beautiful hair at all - just let it flow and float around them.

Nia was noticing all this when Sirena said:

"Now, Nia, if you are ready, we will begin our journey to our home. But it's a long way, and we must keep together, so I will have to guide you," and she held out her hand to Nia.

"Okay," answered Nia, and took the mermaids hand extended to her with a trustful smile, and as soon as they held hands, they began to descend down through the water, and it grew quite dark for a time.

Nia, looked all around as they travelled and soon began to notice the water lighten again and that they seemed to be coming into brighter parts of the ocean.

"Are there roads in the ocean?" she asked, swimming swiftly beside her two new friends.

"Oh, yes, of course. At the bottom, on the ocean floor, there are roads," replied Sirena. "But we are higher up in the water now, so we don't need to travel by road, unless—"

She seemed to hesitate, so Nia asked, "Unless what?"

"Unless we meet with some unfriendly creatures," said Coralia. "It's not quite as safe up here compared to the very bottom. That's the reason we are holding your hand."

"You mean like sharks?" asked Nia anxiously.

"Well, yes, sharks may be dangerous to you," replied Sirena, "but just stay near us. They would never bite a mermaid, and sure if any come by they will just think you are a mermaid too, so don't worry Nia, we won't let anything in the ocean injure us, and we will protect you."

Nia was thoughtful for a few moments and looked around her a little anxiously. Now and then a dark form shot across their pathway or passed them some distance away, but she couldn't tell exactly what they were.

Suddenly they swam right into a huge school of fish, and Nia knew what they were. Yellowtail snappers! Hundreds of them and big ones too! When they saw Sirena and Coralia, they moved away to the side and opened a path for Nia and the mermaids to pass through.

"Will they hurt us?" asked Nia.

"No," laughed Coralia. "Fishes are usually friendly, and this family is quite harmless."

"Never fear," said Sirena, "We'll take very good care of you!"

"Is there any creature I should be afraid of?" asked the young girl.

"One or two, I suppose," answered Sirena. "But don't worry, we mermaids have great powers and can protect you."

"What about sea snakes?" asked Nia, worried now.

"We know the sea snakes very well, and we like them," said Sirena softly.

"You do!" exclaimed Nia.

"Oh, yes. They're very kind. Land people don't seem to like them very much. I suppose it's because they are not too nice to look at, but they are kind to us and much loved."

"How much further do we have to go?"

"Are you getting tired?" Sirena asked.

"Oh no," said Nia, "I'm just excited to see what your houses look like."

"Well, we're nearly there. We're certainly hundreds of miles from the cave where we started," she told her.

"What! Hundreds of miles?" Nia exclaimed in wonder.

"Yes, and we are nearing our home. We need to go down a bit now because we live at the very bottom of the ocean and in its deepest part. Okay?"

CHAPTER 4
THE MERMAID'S HOME

The water grew a deep blue as they descended further into the depths of the ocean and further away from the rays of the sun. But as they descended farther down towards the ocean floor, Nia was surprised to find that it was not at all as dark or gloomy as she had expected. Things were not quite as clear to her as they had been in the bright sunshine above the ocean's surface or in the water as they swam earlier, but every object was clear nevertheless. It was like she was looking at everything through a green glass bottle. And really, it seemed to Nia that they were approaching a beautiful city.

The very bottom of the ocean was covered in white sand, on which stood strangely shaped buildings built of coral; white, pink and yellow. There seemed to be no windows in any of the buildings, and big archways served as doors. And around the buildings, grew many varieties of tall sea shrubs that looked just like small trees that you would see on land. But unlike the trees on the land, here the branches and leaves were all sorts of gorgeous colours - all vivid shades of pink, purple, red, orange and yellow and blue.

Nia watched it all in amazement. Then she saw, at a little distance, she could make out underwater houses and caves and streets, swarming with beautiful mermaids and handsomely dressed mermen; some hurrying this way, others swimming that way. The whole place was a whirlpool of merpeople, fish, and sea creatures. Lots looked busy and were rushing along. And now and then, there were several mermaids reclining on couches of coral, all beautifully dressed and wearing sparkling jewels. Nia watched the little merchildren playing with tiny seahorses. She could hear singing to, at almost every turn, and the mermaids sang songs so beautiful they filled Nia with joy.

She barely knew where to look. Everywhere, there was colour and splendour.

"You live here?" Nia asked.

"Yes, all the merpeople live here," answered Sirena.

"It's very beautiful," Nia said.

"It is isn't it. We love our ocean home so much," said Coralia.

"Are there many more mermaids beside you?" asked Nia.

"Thousands," said Sirena.

"And mermen!" added Coralia.

"Wait, who are they?" Nia asked when she noticed several large fish with long spikes on their noses.

"Those are swordfish," Sirena answered.

"Are they dangerous?" asked Nia.

"Not to us," said Coralia. "The swordfish are our police, and they guard the entrances to the city and gardens which surround our homes. They are very brave and fast and carry a strong weapon. If any creatures try to enter uninvited, the swordfish stop them and make sure they know their way, or send them away."

Nia saw how the swordfishes swords were sharp and strong, and imagined they would be very good at their job.

The three friends now headed into a wide road towards their house and the swordfishes made way for them to pass, afterwards going back to their posts with watchful eyes.

As the three friends slowly swam along the avenue, Nia noticed how the ocean bed was carpeted with colourful sea flowers that looked like the orchids her mom loved so much. The houses of the merpeople were all glowing with lights as they approached, and Nia was amazed at the sight.

"How do you get lights under the sea?" she asked.

"From electric jellyfish and glow-worms, but the jellyfish are the best," the mermaids said. "We have many of them in our homes, as you will see."

Finally, they came to a stop outside a pretty building of pink coral. They paused just before an archway.

"We're here!" said Coralia in her sweet voice. "I hope you will like our home!"

"Yes. Shall we go in?"

"Come on, then," said Coralia, and once more taking Nia's hand, she led the girl through an archway and into a large room, while Sirena followed just behind them.

Nia soon found herself in a house that was very beautiful indeed. The rooms had walls of pink and white coral, and sure enough, electric jellyfish acted as a chandelier on the ceiling of all the rooms making them as bright and cheerful as day. Nia watched these beautiful, curious creatures with delight, for she had only ever known jellyfish to be dangerous and sting.

All the walls were covered with shimmering mother-of-pearl shells, and embroidered coloured seaweed curtains draped across as doorways. Pictures of sea life in frames made of mother of pearl lined the walls, and cushions of soft, white sponges lay on the couches. Also in the room where things Nia recognised like tables, mirrors, ornaments and many articles used by land people like her and her mom, which later at lunch, the mermaids told her had been salvaged from sunken ships. But just at that moment, as Nia and the mermaids entered the room, they found the mermaid's mother reclining on a couch before an air fountain that was sending thousands of tiny bubbles up through the water.

"Oh good, you're back," said their mother, smiling. "and look, Zale, we have a visitor."

"Hi mother, this is Nia," said the mermaids.

"Welcome Nia, I am Sirena and Coralia's mother, and this is their brother Zale."

Zale was young and handsome with hair as dark as Sirena's and blue eyes.

"And this is perfect timing, as Zale has just had his hair cut and Lobster is now leaving." their mother continued.

Just then, a huge lobster said, "Excuse me," then went swimming past, and as it left, it turned around, shook its claw at the family and swam away.

"Have you had anything to eat?" the mother then asked.

"No mother, we haven't eaten a thing since breakfast, and I am starving," said Coralia.

The mermaid's mother insisted that the girls have something to eat before they went exploring any further, and so Nia, Sirena and Coralia lay upon couches so that they could rest after their long swim and just chat.

Nia couldn't sit down as she normally would, because of her mermaid tail; but she joined Sirena and Coralia and they floated down and rested very gracefully upon the couches with their tails touching the floor.

"I think I'll go get you something, what would you like?" asked the mermaid's mother. "Zale is a wonderful cook, so he can help me make something for you."

"Cook?" cried Nia. "How can you cook in the water?"

"Well that's easy, we use the sun's rays for cooking anything we want," was the reply.

"But what if it's a cloudy day, and the sun doesn't shine?" asked Nia.

"Then we eat salads or use hot springs that bubble up in another part of the ocean," Sirena answered. "But the sun is the best."

"And sometimes if we're stuck we can get electricity from the Electric Ray's. They are clumsy fish, but very helpful and have loads of electric power," said Zale.

As the three girls waited for their food to arrive, the mermaids combed their hair with brushes made of polished tortoise-shell and sang pretty songs. Then the mermaids brushed Nia's hair and tied it with ribbons of red and green seaweed. Nia loved every minute.

Soon Zale and the mermaid's mother came into the room with trays of hot food, seaweed, and other sea fruit which they placed upon a large table in the shape of a shell, that was covered in a table cloth made of woven seaweed. Nia and the mermaids each took some, and with plenty to eat, and they all ate cheerfully because they were really hungry.

Nia had no idea what she was eating, but it was yummy and hot, and the young girl found the fruits delicious to eat. The mermaid's mother was pleased when Nia asked for more.

While they ate, Nia soon found herself answering a great many questions about her life on the land, for a while the mermaids kept track of what was going on on the land, there were many things about human life they didn't know, and they were very interested. Nia told them all about what it is like to live on land, all the animals like elephants and tigers and bears. Her stories were so funny that everybody laughed.

Soon the conversation turned to life underwater.

"Do you like what you've seen so far of our life in the ocean?" asked Zale.

"I do," answered Nia.

"Well, now that you are here," continued the mother in a friendly tone, "you are very welcome to stay as long as you like, and see more of the wonderful sights of our ocean."

"I would like that," said Nia, "I'd like it very much, but I need to get back to my mom, she would worry if I don't get back soon."

"You don't need to worry about that," said the mother with a smile.

"Why?" asked Nia.

"Well, because time is different in the ocean, so she will not even realise how long you are away. And I can see that she is not worrying at the moment."

"You can see that?" inquired Nia.

"Of course. Very easily. I can see that just at the moment your mom is sitting on her towel on the beach and reading a magazine." The mermaid's mother said. Then she paused for a second before adding:

"Now you're mother is taking a small nap, and instead of worries, I promise you that she is having happy dreams."

"Wow!" exclaimed Nia in delight.

"And now," said the mermaid's mother, "Why don't you go for a swim with Sirena and Coralia, who will show you some of the wonderful sights of our ocean."

"We'll take you to the most interesting parts of the ocean, where the largest and most remarkable sea creatures live. And we must visit Chester, too, because the old sea turtle would feel hurt if we didn't bring our land visitor to see him," said Coralia.

"That will be nice," said Nia eagerly.

CHAPTER 5

CHESTER

Nia and her two mermaids friends left the house and found themselves in the pretty ocean flower gardens. Coloured shrimps, prawns, and crabs swam amongst gorgeous sea-anemones of all shapes, sizes and bright colours.

Immediately, a school of gorgeous orange and white butterflyfish darted past. "Good morning!" they called to the mermaids as they passed.

"Let's go this way to the jellyfish," said Coralia excited to show their land visitor all of her favourite things.

First, they passed over a carpet of sea flowers, the colourful blossoms swaying on their stems with the motion of the water as they swam past. They had not gone very far when they came to a clearing, and they stopped for a moment to watch a big bloom of beautifully coloured jellyfish floating in the clear water. Nia had never seen anything like it and was mesmerised. The jellyfish made of beautiful shapes. Some were clear, but others were shining in vibrant colours of pink, yellow, blue, and purple.

"How beautiful!" exclaimed Nia, delighted.

She had only ever seen jellyfish when they wash up on the shore and she never ever went near them in case they would sting. Whereas, here in their ocean home, they appeared delicate and gentle.

"Careful not to touch Nia!" warned Sirena, "They may look lovely, but they are just as dangerous to you here as they are on land."

Next Nia and the mermaids went to visit Chester. They had gone a little way when Sirena said "There he is! Bet he wants to see our land visitor."

"Who? Where?" asked Nia anxiously, for she was a little frightened thinking she could get hurt somehow after what Sirena had told her about the jellyfish.

Just then Nia looked up and saw a startling sight. A huge shape floated above her, and the head was connected to a huge shell.

"Hi Chester," said Coralia, following Nia's gaze.

"Won't he hurt us?" asked Nia with a shiver of fear.

"Who, Chester? Oh no! He's our next-door neighbour, and he may be grumpy, but he's as gentle as anything."

"Can he talk?" asked Nia.

"Perfectly," replied Chester. "I am right here, you know, I may not have ears like yours, but I can hear you talking about me, and I think it's very rude."

"Oh, I'm sorry. I hope you well?" said Sirena.

"Quite well, thank you," answered Chester,

Nia floated around staring at him, for she had never seen a turtle up close before, and didn't know quite what to make of it. Almost without thinking, she reached forward and stroked the shining shell that the strange creature wore on its back. The movement, gentle though it was, startled the large turtle. With one sweep he turned in her direction, then said:

"Are you from the land people?"

"Yes, my name is Nia," she answered.

And as she looked into his face, she decided he was not at all scary. He had a serious look on his face, and his nose was flat, but his eyes were dark and kind. He had a long, olive green shell and his flippers moved gently back and forth.

"The last land person I knew was Charles Darwin."

"Oh no, you didn't," said Nia, because she knew all about Charles Darwin - she had learnt about him in school, and he had lived in the 1800s!

"He lived over one hundred years ago and was the first to discover how living things survive. Were you alive, then?" she asked.

"Yes," said Chester.

"How old are you?" inquired Nia curiously.

"No one knows. I've been here for years. I used to visit the land a lot, but when I overheard them threaten to make me into soup or put me in a zoo I came here, and I stay here now because I've learned to like the water better than the land. Perhaps I'm two hundred years old, perhaps more. I often lose track of the centuries down here in the ocean. I'm certainly not as old as Bowhead," he answered.

"Bowhead?" asked Nia.

"Yes, Bowhead is an arctic whale, he's well over two hundred years old and has some fascinating stories to tell about the whalers 200 years ago," said Coralia.

"How old are mermaids?" asked Nia, looking at the mermaids and wonderingly. They seemed young and just like her.

"Merpeople have existed for many thousands of years," said Coralia with pride. "But Sirena and I are just about the same age as you."

Nia and the mermaids spent time chatting to Chester about all of the interesting things he had seen in his long life. When it was time to leave and continue on their adventure, Nia was sad to say goodbye.

Next Nia and the mermaids went past two stately swordfishes standing guard who let them past, and then they were out in the wide ocean.

CHAPTER 6
THE INKY CUTTLEFISH

Now that they had left the city, the three swam slowly along, enjoying the cold depths of the water. Every so often they met with some strange creature—or one that seemed strange to Nia— because while she had seen many kinds of fish in the sea, in aquariums on the TV, in books and on the internet, it was very different meeting them face to face.

The big fish she was swimming alongside were certainly not at all like the kinds she had seen in the supermarket or struggling at the end of a fishing line or flopping from a net at the pier. And while she knew the taste, as well as the look, of plaice and salmon, sole and dab, she really did not know much about their life in the ocean.

They passed all kinds of fish swimming around free and happy in their deep-sea home. Often they would find themselves swimming amid schools of fish swimming all around them in the water with marvellous activity. As Nia and the mermaids swan near them, the fish just harmlessly darted away.

Soon, they spotted a group of large codfish lying lazily near the bottom of the sea. They were a dark colour on their backs with silver underneath, and the only motion they made was the movement of their fins and gills.

"Quick codfish," said Sirena.

"Are they dangerous?" asked Nia.

"No, not at all. But we don't want to scare them. They don't like people from the land because the fishermen have caught so many over the years that to be truthful, there's not many left," answered Sirena.

"They're barely moving," said Nia.

"That's okay. We don't mind if they're lazy because then they're less likely to be caught," said Coralia.

"AHH! What's that?!" exclaimed Nia, trembling as she was pointing downward. One minute there was nothing there, and the next she saw a huge red monster with two large eyes, two long tentacles and what looked like eight long arms coming out of its head! And it was coming straight towards them! Then, all at once, it grew dark around them. Nia didn't like it one bit, and it made her more nervous not to be able to see what was going on around her or where the creature might be.

"That is a cuttlefish," answered Sirena after a glance ahead of them, "we didn't see him at first because he was camouflaged and now he's dyeing the water around him with ink so that he can hide from us. Quick, turn to the right, for we will not be able to see anything at all in that inky water."

Following her advice, they made a quick curve to the right, and at once, the water began to lighten again in that direction.

"How does the cuttlefish make the water so dark?"

"They carry big sacks of ink in front of them," Sirena answered. "Then, whenever they feel like it - they can shoot the ink out into the water around them."

The three friends kept swimming, and soon the inky water was far behind them.

On and on they travelled through the underwater world, full at every turn with curious, beautiful, and incredible sights. Sometimes, Nia saw fairyland like forests of kelp and seaweed gently waving in the tide with bright-coloured fish making them all the more beautiful.

Other times, the bed of the ocean was as smooth as her own kitchen floor, and the water as clear as crystal, while the white sandy bottom acted as a reflector to the bright sunshine above the surface.

In some places, there were large areas of stumpy, scrubby marine vegetation like seaweed, and of a bluish-grey tinge, clumps of spongy fan-shaped fungi, which when dried in the sun look beautiful.

But to Nia, the most wonderful sights where when they swam amongst the different types of fish. Goldfish and silverfish darted here and there, and the whole scene was so pretty and peaceful that Nia began to doubt there was even any danger lurking in such a lovely place. Her favourites were the striking blue and yellow Emperor Angelfish; and cheerily coloured round balls that floated gently in the water, that the mermaids told her were called

Balloonfish. They looked so cute with their little eyes and mouths.

"They do look like cute balloons but watch out! They have little spikes all over them so that their enemies won't bite them for fear of getting pricked."

"Wow! look there," said Coralia." we're right on top of a nice little family of sharks."

Nia looked down, and sure enough, lying closely together on a bottom of the sand and coral were about ten sharks, heads and tails all in a perfect line, and lying perfectly still until they heard the mermaids and then they moved on.

"I thought sharks couldn't stop swimming?" wondered Nia. "But they looked like they were sleeping."

Nia knew sharks were powerful and fierce hunters and had heard lots of stories about people being attacked with their seven rows of sharp teeth!

"That's right Nia, lots of sharks have to swim constantly to keep oxygen-rich water flowing over their gills. But there are lots of different kinds of sharks, and these are lemon sharks, look at their colour - yellow and brown."

CHAPTER 7
OCTAVIUS

As the day wore on, Nia realised that living on land she had no idea of life in the deep ocean.

"Oh no, look out," said Coralia in a low voice. "It's Octi."

Nia quickly looked around just as a giant long brown arm stretched across their way in front, and another just behind them, as the octopus himself came slowly sliding up to them.

"Com' on, Octi please, let us by!" said Coralia. "We are not in the mood for your games."

"Games? Me?!" said the octopus with a laugh. "Well, well. Who do we have here?" he continued. "I don't believe I have met this new neighbour?"

"Octi please let us past," said Coralia, beginning to get angry as two more unwanted legs covered in round suckers tangled around them.

"Let's us go," shouted Nia. "I don't like octopuses."

"*OctoPI!*" said the creature, correcting her, and entangling her in two more arms twisting and writhing like snakes. With his tough, knobbly brownish skin, large staring eyes, his parrot's beak, and ugly bag of a body, Nia thought that the huge octopus was a horrid-looking creature. While she struggled to untangle herself, the octopus just laughed at her and pulled his arms tighter. Nia became frightened, and he just laughed even more.

"You're being rude," she declared when, with the help of the mermaids, she finally broke free.

"What!" cried the octopus laughing and entangling the mermaids and Nia in yet another two arms.

"Let us go!" persisted all three.

"I'm just having fun?" he said grumpily, and it was easy to see he was offended.

"You know it's no wonder, up on the land, where I live, people eat octopus," said Nia.

"Stop!" cried the octopus in a shocked tone voice. "Do you mean to tell me that you are a land person?"

"Yes," said Nia positively.

"Oh, no!" moaned the octopus, quickly withdrawing his arms and dropping his head, and Nia thought she could actually see tears falling down his cheeks.

"What's the matter?" she asked gently because annoying as he was, she really didn't like to see the octopus upset.

"It's cruel!" sobbed the octopus sadly. "We are just as clever as you land people. Just because we have more long arms and don't live like you, you catch us and — oh, I can't say it! It's too horrible, too humiliating!"

"Come, let's go," said Sirena. So they left poor Octi weeping and went on their way. With that, the octopus did a quick backward swim and blasted through the water away from them, his arms trailing behind.

"I'm not a bit sorry for him," said Coralia, "he's always catching us in his arms and it's annoying."

"He is very annoying," said Sirena, "but he's very clever too. Did you know that an octopus has eight brains?! Once there was a shipwreck near here, and we found glass jam jars and Octi was the only one who could open them without breaking them. And did you know he can walk?"

"Really, he can walk?" asked Nia.

"Yes, and he's just about the best camouflager in the whole ocean," replied

Coralia. "It does seem wrong that land people capture and eat octopus. He hasn't been up to the land for many, many, years."

"Well, I promise that from now on, I will never *ever* eat octopus again?" said Nia.

"I'm glad of that," said Sirena.

CHAPTER 8
SYLVESTER

The three friends continued swimming until they were as far away from land as possible and then Nia, Sirena and Coralia ascended up through the water, and soon they were near the top of the ocean. The three popped their heads above the water. And Nia found herself looking up at the clear sky for the first time since she had started on this magical adventure. She floated in the water, with her head and face just out of it, Sirena and Coralia were at her side.

Looking around, they could see that the ocean was very quiet. A gentle breeze was blowing, and the sky was a clear light blue fringed at the horizon with peaceful clouds.

Suddenly Nia heard a long mournful sound. As she listened, other sounds - the same but in different tones - joined in until it sounded like hundreds of voices saying one long-drawn-out single word "Hel-l-o-o-o-wwww" over and over again.

Then, all of a sudden, there was a strange motion in the water.

"What's the matter?" Nia said, "what's that noise?"

"Whales, and they're close. We'll wait until the rise again," Sirena answered.

"Any minute now," Coralia murmured softly.

Silently the girls waited, treading water and rocking lazily with the gentle swell of the ocean, and sure enough, not half a mile away, was a burst of water rising up from the ocean, and just then, they caught sight of a gigantic shape rising out of the water then dipping down again out of sight.

"It's Sylvester," said Sirena.

"Who's Sylvester?" Nia asked.

"Only the biggest Blue Whale and best rollercoaster in the ocean!" said Coralia excitedly.

Nia only just heard her in time to turn her head and wonder what the mermaid meant when suddenly the powerful animal jumped and swept clean over their heads.

Now Nia could see how huge the strange monster of the deep was. It was shaped like a fish and had a great head, a huge mouth, large enough to swallow a boat. It was by far the biggest animal Nia had ever seen, and she was scared.

"Won't he swallow us up?" Nia asked.

"Not at all. Whales eat about a ton of food every day, but it's mostly fish, and certainly not merpeople or land people." answered Sirena.

"They swim through the ocean with their big mouths gaping open, and thousands of little creatures float inside," said Coralia.

In spite of all assurances, Nia was worried.

Just then a huge whale came dashing up.

"Why, what are you doing here?" said the whale, surprised.

"Sylvester, this is Nia, our land visitor, and we are showing her around our world," said Coralia.

"A land visitor, well, pleased to meet you, Nia," the whale nodded his great head in greeting.

"Pleased to meet you too," Nia replied. "You are by far the biggest fish I have ever met."

"I am not a fish; I am a mammal, like you," said Sylvester.

When he spoke, his great tongue came forward, pushing out all the seawater from his mouth.

"What do you mean, like me?" asked a surprised Nia, for she certainly didn't think she looked like a whale!

"Well I look like a fish, but I have no gills, like fish, to take air from the water. I breathe air like you, and I have a backbone and hair on my body like you. You and I are both mammals. But of course, I do not live on land."

Well, well, nature is full of surprises thought Nia. It is shaped like a fish, and its home is in the sea, so no wonder it has often been called a fish. Isn't it is very strange that the largest member of the whole animal kingdom should live in the ocean?

"Wow," said Nia. "do you like living in the ocean?"

"I do. I can travel all over the world and have seen many things, steamers, sailing ships, trailers, and I have a large family and good friends," he said. " We live a happy life, though not without dangers. It hasn't always been easy - over the centuries we have often been hunted for our oil."

"Please can we have a ride, Sylvester?" asked Coralia.

"Well, the others are waiting for me, but perhaps just one would be alright. Perhaps Nia would like it."

The mermaids spun in the water laughing with happiness. Then, as they held hands, there was a bump, and suddenly Nia and the mermaids were flying through the air on top of the enormous whale. When they shot high up into the air and went back down into the water, the whale raised his gigantic tail up and thrashed the water with deafening blows, rolling at the same time from side to side until the surrounding sea was white with froth. Nia and the mermaids laughed with joy as they were tossed around and around.

After they had had their fun, the whale broke water once again, but this time he was some distance off. The girls waved, and Sylvester replied with a huge jet of water out of his blowhole as he swam away in the opposite direction.

CHAPTER 9
TURTLE ISALAND

Nia and the mermaids continued to swim, this time towards a small island and now the ocean was azure under the rays of the sun.

Blue dolphins full of fun, almost the same size as Nia, whizzed past, leaping and bounding into the air, as they chased flying fish for dinner. Warm summer sun's rays warmed her face when she popped out of the water to look around, but she didn't suffer from the heat, because she stayed in the cold water. The island waters teemed with fish she recognised as mackerel.

Soon, rising near the small rocky desert island, at first, they heard the barking, then they saw dozens of furry seals lying asleep or sunning themselves on the rocks, while baby seals waddled and a shuffled around as they played.

Swimming closer to the rocks, Nia saw hundreds of coloured starfish lying on the bottom, with their six points extended outward, and as Nia looked down into the blue water, she thought they looked like the stars in the sky on a moonlit night.

"Starfish like to keep close to the shore," said Sirena.

"And lookout for the little seahorses you love so much. They live near the coast, and they love the weeds."

Sure enough, Nia saw the strange little

seahorse fish. She held out her hand and a little brown fish with a curved neck settled in her palm that looked just like a knight on the chess-board. Letting it go again to join the others it was fun to watch them play hide-and-seek using their little twisty monkey tails to cling to the seaweed.

Closer to the rocks, they watched crabs tumble over each other as they scrambled over the rocks to meet their cousins - bright orange lobsters,"

"They're very smart creatures too you know," said Coralia,

"Like Octi?" asked Nia.

"Yep, like Octi. There are many smart creatures in the sea, like dolphins, orcas and otters."

The rock pools left by the tide had many interesting things to show Nia - lots of living creatures - shrimps, prawns and crabs and shells, besides the pretty weeds, with anemones and shellfish of all kinds. There were also unusual tiny little fish, nearly invisible in the glinting light and shadows of the rock pools, who made quick movements and darted away when Nia put her hand near them.

Moving on, they soon they came to a sandy beach and watched as swarms of green turtles scooped out holes in the sand with their flippers to lay their eggs in the sand.

One of the turtles must have heard them, looked up and then quickly withdrew its legs and heads into its thick shell.

"It's okay, we won't hurt you," said Coralia gently.

The turtle sneaked another peak and then tried to turn its short legs struggling to turn around, then when it reached the shore, it jumped into the water and shot off with remarkable swiftness.

But as they came closer to the other turtles, the gentle voices and touch of the mermaids made them friendly and tame.

The three girls lay with their tails in the water gentle waves and watched great flocks of seagulls, whirling in the air, overhead.

They had seen many amazing sights in the ocean that afternoon, and Nia thoroughly enjoyed their glimpse of sea life.

Sirena and Coralia had been good friends to their young land guest, and it had been an amazing adventure. The day had been long and adventurous, and they had travelled far, but Nia was starting to get tired, and she missed her mom.

"What time is it?" asked Nia.

"We know nothing of time," said Sirena. "Would you like to go back to our mermaid home for a while or would you rather go back to Smuggler's Cave?"

"Well, I guess I'd better go back home," decided Nia. "I think its best. I mean, I've been away a while, and I would like to see my mom."

"Very well," replied Sirena. "Let us turn in that direction, then."

Nia took one last view of the island, and the next moment she was in the vast ocean again, swimming towards Smuggler's Cave beside her two mermaid friends.

It was time to return home.

CHAPTER 10
HOME TO DRY LAND

Away they swam, fast through the blue-green ocean, passed schools of fishes all shouting goodbye to the young visitor from the land. The mermaids used their magic power to travel across the ocean in super quick time, and before Nia knew it, she was home.

"Here's the ocean entrance Smuggler's Cave," said Sirena.

"What, already?" asked Nia happily, for she was anxious to see her mom now. Then they swam through the dark water, passed through the rocky entrance, and began to ascend slowly into the turquoise-blue water of the cave.

Cautiously, they pushed their heads above the turquoise water and looked around the cave. It was silent and deserted, so they floated gently to the very spot where they had set off on their journey sometime earlier, and Nia turned an inquiring face toward the mermaids.

"Just climb out," said Coralia.

So she pulled herself up and awkwardly tumbled onto the rock. As she did, her mermaid tail disappeared, and she was back to herself again.

"We hope you enjoyed your visit with us," said Sirena, smiling up at her new land friend.

"Oh, I did. It was the best day ever, and I will always remember this as long as I live," exclaimed Nia.

Sirena was thoughtful for a moment, then she pulled a tiny ring from one of her fingers, a plain gold band set with one small pearl, and gave it to the Nia.

"If at any time we can help you Nia," she said, "come to the edge of the ocean and call my name. If you are wearing this ring at the time, I shall instantly hear you and come to you."

"Thank you!" cried Nia, slipping the ring over her little finger, which it fitted perfectly. "I will never forget you."

"Goodbye, Nia!" they called.

"Goodbye!" shouted Nia, and she blew two kisses from her fingers toward the mermaids as they swam away, then turning a small way off, to wave, their silky hair floating around them. Then, suddenly, the faces disappeared, leaving ripples on the surface of the turquoise water.

Nia picked up her float and started toward the mouth of the cave and back to her mom. She blinked as she came out into the bright sunlight and took a deep breath of fresh air. What a journey she had had, but it was good to breathe the fresh air again and go out into the warm sunshine. She smiled with happiness at seeing her world again.

The End

Have you read

The Fox in the Suitcase Series?

ABOUT THE AUTHOR

Stephanie O'Connor is an Irish writer of novels and short stories for children and adults. She grew up in Bangor Co, Down, Northern Ireland. After university, she moved to Boston, US, for almost ten years before returning to Ireland where she now lives in beautiful Co Wicklow, Ireland, with her husband and their two children. When Stephanie isn't working or writing stories she likes to read, paint and spend time with family and friends.

Find out more at
www.stephanieoconnorbooks.com

Printed in Great Britain
by Amazon

76182900R00059